THE BRUMBACK LIBRARY
OF VAN WERT COUNTY
VAN WERT, OHIO

WORD BIRD'S
THANKSGIVING WORDS

by Jane Belk Moncure

illustrated by Linda Hohag

Created by

THE
CHILD'S
WORLD

Distributed by CHILDRENS PRESS ®
Chicago, Illinois

CHILDRENS PRESS HARDCOVER EDITION
ISBN 0-516-06577-7

CHILDRENS PRESS PAPERBACK EDITION
ISBN 0-516-46577-5

Library of Congress Cataloging in Publication Data

Moncure, Jane Belk.
    Word Bird's Thanksgiving words.

    (Word house words for early birds)
    Summary: Word Bird puts words about Thanksgiving in
his word house—Pilgrims, Indian corn, wigwam, pumpkin
pie, and others.
    1. Vocabulary—Juvenile literature.   2. Thanksgiving
Day—Juvenile literature.   [1. Vocabulary.
2. Thanksgiving Day]   I. Hohag, Linda, ill.   II. Title.
III. Series: Moncure, Jane Belk.   Word house words for
early birds.
PE1449.M5335   1987   394.2'683   86-32639
ISBN 0-89565-360-5

1 2 3 4 5 6 7 8 9 10 11 12 R 95 94 93 92 91 90 89 88 87

WORD BIRD'S
THANKSGIVING WORDS

Word Bird made a ...

word house.

"I will put Thanksgiving words in my house," he said.

He put in these words—

Mayflower

The Pilgrims' Landing

Plymouth Rock

Pilgrims

Samoset   Squanto

Indians

Indian homes

Indian corn

Pilgrim harvest

The First Thanksgiving

The First Thanksgiving

Pilgrim hats

"Pilgrims"

Indian hats

wigwam

Indian foods

Indian words

Indian tom-toms

Indian dance

Thanksgiving basket

turkey

pumpkin pie

Thanksgiving party

Word Bird's Thankful Words

Family

Home

Friends

School

giving thanks

28

Can you read these

Mayflower

Indian corn

Plymouth Rock

Pilgrim harvest

Pilgrims

The First Thanksgiving

Indians

Pilgrim hats

Indian homes

"Pilgrims"

Thanksgiving words with Word Bird ?

Indian hats

Indian dance

wigwam

Thanksgiving basket

Indian foods

corn
squash
beans

turkey

Indian words

moccasin
moose
papoose

pumpkin pie

Indian tom-toms

Thanksgiving party

31

You can make a Thanksgiving word house. You can put Word Bird's words in your house and read them too.

Can you think of other Thanksgiving words to put in your word house?